W9-AHX-915

The Boxcar Children Mysteries

THE PUMPKIN HEAD MYSTERY
created by
GERTRUDE CHANDLER WARNER

Illustrated by Robert Papp

ALBERT WHITMAN & Company
Chicago, Illinois

The Pumpkin Head Mystery
Created by Gertrude Chandler Warner;
Illustrated by Robert Papp.

ISBN: 978-0-8075-6668-8 (hardcover)
ISBN: 978-0-8075-6669-5 (paperback)

10 9 8 7 6 5 4 3 2 1 LB 15 14 13 12 11 10

Cover art by Robert Papp.

For information about Albert Whitman & Company,
visit our web site at www.albertwhitman.com.

Contents

THE PUMPKIN HEAD MYSTERY

CHAPTER 1

A Pumpkin Head Ghost

"How does it look?" asked Jessie, stepping down from the ladder. She stood on the lawn and looked up at the fall decorations on Grandfather's big white house.

"It's very pretty," said ten-year-old Violet. She tied a yellow ribbon to a pot of purple mums. Purple was Violet's favorite color. She placed the pot next to the front door.

"Nice job, Jessie," said Henry. "I will put the ladder away for you when I am done here." Henry was hammering a post into the ground. At fourteen, Henry was the oldest of the four Alden children. "That feels nice and sturdy," he said. "Are you ready, Benny?"

Henry, Jessie, and Violet looked down at six-year-old Benny. They burst out laughing. Their little brother was covered in straw from head to toe. He was stuffing an old pair of pants and shirt.

"I can't tell which one is the scarecrow and which one is Benny," said Henry.

Benny jumped up. "I am Benny!" he cried. "And this is Sam. But he's not done yet."

"Let me help," said Jessie. Jessie was twelve and often acted like a mother to her younger brother. She pinned Sam's shirt to his pants. She struggled to button all the buttons on the bulging shirt.

"Sam sure is a fat scarecrow," said Violet.

"I stuffed him with a lot of straw," said Benny. "I didn't want him to be hungry."

Violet smiled. "Scarecrows don't get hungry," she said.

"But I sure do!" Benny cried. Benny was famous for his big appetite.

Henry patted the round stomach of the scarecrow. "If only it were that easy to fill up Benny!" he said. Henry began to tie the scarecrow to the post.

"Wait!" Benny cried. "Sam doesn't have a head yet. What can I use to make a head?"

"How about a pumpkin head?" asked Henry. "We could carve a face into it and light a candle inside it at night."

"Cool idea!" Benny cried. "That would be spooky!"

"I would like some pumpkins to decorate the front porch, too," Jessie said.

Just then Grandfather drove up the driveway. "The house looks terrific," he called out the open window. The four Aldens were orphans. After their parents died, they ran away and lived in an abandoned boxcar in the woods. Their grandfather found them and brought them to live with him in his big house in Greenfield.

"Do you like my scarecrow, Grandfather?" Benny asked. "I named him Sam. But we need to find a pumpkin to make his head. I'm going to make him a spooky scarecrow."

"Well, would you like to come with me?" Grandfather asked. "I am on my way to visit old friends of mine, George and Mae Beckett. They have a farm. I am sure that they have pumpkins for sale."

"We'd love to," Jessie said. She brushed the straw from Benny's clothes and the children piled into Grandfather's car.

After a short ride, Grandfather turned onto a dirt lane. A sign by the road read *Beckett Farm: Hayrides, Pumpkins, Flowers, and Fresh Farm Vegetables for Sale*. The sign was crooked. It looked as though it might fall over.

"That's odd," said Grandfather. "That was a new sign. George put it up just last year. I wonder what happened to it?"

They drove up the lane. "What a beautiful place," Violet said. Fields and hills surrounded them. The leaves on the trees were turning bright shades of yellow and orange and red.

Grandfather parked the car on a gravel lot next to a farm stand. "This looks like the perfect place for you children to pick out some pumpkins. Why don't you look around? I will go find my friends."

The farm stand had pumpkins and pots of flowers for sale.

"There are so many flowers!" Violet said, looking at the display racks. A small goat stuck its head through a fence. It tried to nibble on the flowers.

"Look at that horse over there," Henry said. "It is as black as midnight." The beautiful mare grazed on the grass in a nearby field.

Jessie admired the colorful autumn wreaths. "Look, Henry. Wouldn't this be nice on the front door?" she asked.

A loud groan made them turn quickly. Benny was standing in a pile of pumpkins. He was trying to lift one of the biggest ones. His face was quite red.

"Stop that! Get away from there!" An angry woman shouted from a small booth at the back of the farm stand. She walked out of the booth and straight up to Benny. "What

do you think you are doing?" she asked accusingly.

Jessie hurried to her brother's side. "We are only shopping for some pumpkins," she explained. "Is there something wrong?"

The woman put her hands on her hips. She looked carefully at the pumpkins. "If you crack any of these pumpkins open, you must pay for them."

"Of course," Jessie said. "We will be very careful."

"You'd better be!" The woman gave Benny an angry look and walked away.

"I didn't hurt any of the pumpkins," Benny said.

Jessie pulled some straw from Benny's hair. "I know you didn't," she said. She saw the angry woman watching them from beside her booth.

Just then, Grandfather walked across the lawn and waved to the children. "The Becketts would like to meet you," he said. "Come on up to the farmhouse."

Henry, Jessie, Violet, and Benny walked

with Grandfather toward the house.

"It's just like a picture in a magazine!" Violet said. "I wish I had my camera."

A large pumpkin patch stretched out behind the old white house. Next to the house was a big red barn. The Becketts looked like they were the same age as Grandfather. They were sitting on their wide front porch. A delicious aroma floated through the screen door.

"Wow! Something smells really good!" Benny said.

Mrs. Beckett smiled. "That's my apple pie," she said. "I've just taken it out of the oven. It is cooling on the table."

Benny took a long, deep breath. "My nose can almost taste your pie," he said.

Grandfather laughed. "George and Mae, I'd like to introduce you to my grandchildren, Henry, Jessie, Violet, and Benny."

"You have a beautiful farm," Violet said.

"And big pumpkins!" Benny added. "But I didn't hurt any of them."

The Becketts seemed confused. Jessie

explained about the angry woman.

"Oh, George. You should never have let Bessie come back to work at the farm." Mrs. Beckett looked at the Aldens. "We had to fire Bessie last season," she explained. "She has a bad temper. She was not very polite to the customers."

Mr. Beckett's leg was in a big cast. It was propped on a chair. His crutches leaned against the side of the house. "I'm sorry that Bessie was so rude to you, children. She runs the farm stand for me. She should be nice to customers, but sometimes she is not. I can't afford to fire her right now, though. I need the help. It is hard to run a farm with a broken leg."

"That's true," Mrs. Beckett said. "But Bessie has been calling in sick quite a lot lately. She is not as much help as she should be."

"How did you break your leg, George?" asked Grandfather.

Mr. and Mrs. Beckett exchanged a worried glance, then looked at the children.

Just then, a woman with curly red hair marched out of the house onto the porch. "I'll tell you how my father broke his leg. He was chasing after a pumpkin-head ghost in the middle of the night," she said. "Like an old fool."

Benny had been sitting in a small rocking chair. He jumped to his feet. "You have ghosts?" he asked.

Jessie put her arm around her brother. "There are no such things as ghosts," she said.

Mr. Beckett introduced his daughter Sally to the Aldens. "Sally lives in Florida," Mr. Beckett said. "But she is here on the farm for a visit." Then Mr. Beckett turned to Benny. "And your sister, Jessie, is right," he said. "There are no such things as ghosts."

Sally crossed her arms. "Well then what was it that spooked your horse? I thought you said that a pumpkin head ghost..."

"Sally! Please!" Mrs. Beckett looked nervously toward the children.

"Fine." Sally sighed. She flung her purse

over her shoulder. "I am heading into town," she said. "I have a lot to do."

"Please do not go to see Dave Bolger again, Sally," Mr. Beckett said.

"Dad, I have a lot of errands to run. But I might stop in Mr. Bolger's office, too. He is waiting for an answer. And I am, too. You know how much I want you and Mom to come live in Florida."

Mr. Beckett began to shake his head. "Sally, we have already answered you. I'm sorry, but we do not want to move to Florida."

"But your grandchildren hardly ever get to see you!" Sally threw her hands in the air. "And you are both too old to be here alone on this farm. It makes me worry."

Mr. Beckett gripped the arms of his chair. "Sally, we love this farm. And we are perfectly able to take care of it. We are not selling it!"

A man wearing jeans and a flannel shirt walked up to the house. "Tractor's broken again, George," he said. "We'll have to cancel the hayride for the children from the nursery school." Mr. Beckett introduced the man to the Aldens. He was Jason Wylie, a neighbor who also worked on the farm.

"But I just fixed the tractor yesterday," Mr. Beckett said to Jason. "It was working fine this morning."

Jason shrugged. He had a dark oil stain on his hand. When he saw Henry staring at it, he quickly stuffed his hand into his pocket. "Nothing I can do about it," he said. "I don't know anything about tractor engines. Anyway, this is a farm, not a nursery school playground."

Sally turned toward her parents. "See what I mean?" she said. "There is nothing but problems here." She and Jason walked together toward the gravel parking lot. They stood talking next to Sally's car. Sally seemed to be explaining something to Jason. He nodded his head several times. He glanced up at the porch, then quickly turned away.

Mrs. Beckett stood up. "I think we could all use a nice piece of pie," she said. "Is anyone interested?"

"I am!" Benny cried, jumping up. "I'm

starving!"

Jessie shook her head at her little brother.

"I'm sorry. I didn't mean to be rude," Benny said. "I guess I just got excited. The pie smells so good."

Mr. Beckett laughed as he struggled to his feet. "You were not rude. I'm excited, too! My wife makes the best pie in the whole county. You will love it."

Violet handed Mr. Beckett his crutches. Benny rushed to hold the door open.

The old farm kitchen had a wooden floor and a big, round table. The table was covered with a red and white checked tablecloth. The freshly baked pie sat in the center. Jessie set plates out for everyone while Mrs. Beckett made coffee. Henry and Violet filled four tall glasses with milk.

Mrs. Beckett looked tired. She sat at the table and cut big slices of pie for everyone.

Mr. Beckett sat beside his wife. He put his hand over hers. "It was such a bad time to break my leg," he explained. "This is a busy time of year on our farm."

"Yes," said Mrs. Beckett. "In the fall, we have many customers who come here for our haunted hayrides. They buy a lot of pumpkins and flowers, too."

"Haunted hayrides?" Benny looked around the kitchen with wide eyes. "But I thought you said there were no ghosts here."

"They're not *real* ghosts, Benny," Grandfather said.

"It is all for fun," Mr. Beckett explained. "Customers get a hayride in the dark around the farm."

"It sounds scary," said Violet.

"It *is* a little scary, Violet," said Mrs. Beckett. "We hire people to dress up in spooky costumes. But everyone knows it is just pretend. People like to be scared for fun on a haunted hayride. Afterwards, we give out cookies and hot apple cider. And if you don't like to be scared, we have fun hayrides in the daytime, too."

"Wow! This is an awesome farm," Benny said.

"Thank you," said Mr. Beckett. "We do love it here. It is a special place. I don't think we could ever sell it to Dave Bolger."

"Has Dave Bolger made you an offer?" asked Grandfather.

"Yes," Mrs. Beckett said. "He has offered us a lot of money for it. Sally wants us to sell the farm and buy a retirement home in Florida. That way, we could live close to her and our two grandchildren." Mrs. Beckett looked around her cozy kitchen. "But we are not ready to give up our farm."

"And Mr. Bolger will not leave us alone!" Mr. Beckett said. "He makes a new offer every week."

Jessie poured more milk into Benny's glass. "Is Mr. Bolger a farmer, too?" she asked. "He must understand how you feel about your farm."

"No," said Mr. Beckett. "He does not understand. Mr. Bolger is a builder. He bought the Wilson farm next to ours. He built a lot of houses there. Now he wants to buy our farm so he can build more houses." Mr. Beckett looked out the window at his fields.

Mrs. Beckett wiped crumbs from the table. "Our daughter, Sally, might be right about one thing, though," she said. "We have been having a lot of problems lately. And until George gets that cast off his leg, I don't know how we will be able to keep up with things around here."

"We could help," Henry said.

"Yes," Jessie agreed. "We would be happy to help out on your farm."

Mr. Beckett looked surprised. "Farm work can be very hard," he said.

Grandfather smiled. "My grandchildren don't mind hard work. And they like to be helpful."

"That would be wonderful," Mr. Beckett said. "If you're sure you don't mind, we could really use the help."

"We don't mind at all," Violet said.

Suddenly, everyone seemed to be staring at Benny. He was carefully plucking the last little crumbs from his plate. Then he began to lick a small bit of apple from his fork.

"Oh, Benny," Jessie said. "I think you have

gotten it all."

Benny looked up. His face turned red.

Mrs. Beckett hid a small smile. "We do need help around here," she said. "For example, there is one piece of apple pie left. It is too small to save, but I do not like to throw food away."

Benny sat up straight in his chair. "I can help with that!" he said. He held his plate out to Mrs. Beckett.

Grandfather laughed. "When it comes to eating, Benny can always be counted on to help out."

While Grandfather spoke with the Becketts, the children walked back to the farm stand to pick out their pumpkins. Jessie found a few to decorate the front porch. Benny discovered a bright orange one that would be a perfect pumpkin head for his scarecrow.

"I'll carry these to the car," Henry offered.

"I will go pay for them," Violet said. She took the money that Grandfather had given her and walked to the small booth. She did not see Bessie. Violet walked to the side door of the booth and knocked. The door opened slightly when she touched it. Violet saw a roll of tickets, a plate of snacks for sale, and a box with money in it.

"Hello?" she called. But no one was inside. Violet decided to put the money in the cash box. As she left the small booth, she heard someone talking—someone with an angry voice. She could not make out the words. But she saw Bessie standing in the trees on the other side of the field. She seemed to be arguing with a man in a dark suit. Violet hurried back to the car.

Grandfather started the engine and the Aldens headed for home. Violet wondered about what she had seen.

There certainly did seem to be a lot of problems on the Beckett farm.

CHAPTER 2

Farm Stand Trouble

"I can't wait until it is dark!" Benny cried.

"It won't be long now," Jessie said. "I will go find a candle."

Henry lifted the pumpkin head onto the top of the scarecrow. Watch, the Alden's wire-haired terrier, barked excitedly.

"You carved such a scary face into that pumpkin," Violet said. "I don't think Watch likes it very much."

Benny rubbed Watch's head. "Don't worry,

Watch. Sam is just pretend. He is for fun. Scarecrows can't hurt anybody. They can't even move!"

When Jessie came back, she placed a candle inside the pumpkin head. The eerie face glowed in the dark.

"Oh, my! That scarecrow gave me a fright!" Mrs. McGregor, the Aldens' housekeeper, stood on the front lawn. She held a big platter filled with marshmallows, chocolate, and graham crackers. "You have been working so hard out here," she said. "I thought you might like a snack."

"Wow! S'mores!" Benny cried. He jumped up and took the platter from Mrs. McGregor. "Thank you!"

Mrs. McGregor lit a small fire in the fire pit. Soon all four children were toasting marshmallows. Benny made a double-decker sandwich. He piled lots of chocolate and gooey marshmallows between his graham crackers. Just as he opened his mouth to take a big bite, there was a loud screech and a honking horn.

Violet jumped. "What was that?" she asked.

Henry pointed toward the road that ran in front of Grandfather's house. "There was almost a bad accident out there. One car stopped and another one came close to hitting it."

"I wonder why a car would stop in that spot?" Jessie asked. "That's odd."

The drivers shouted at each other, but the children could not hear what they said.

Violet stood up. "I hope everyone is all right."

Finally, both cars drove off. The Aldens watched the two sets of red taillights disappear down the road into the darkness.

"Everything seems to be fine now," Henry said.

After the children finished their s'mores, Henry put out the fire.

Jessie blew out the candle in the pumpkin head. "We should get some rest," she said. "We promised we would be at the Beckett farm early tomorrow morning."

* * *

After a big breakfast of blueberry pancakes made by Mrs. McGregor, Henry, Jessie, Violet, and Benny hopped on their bicycles and rode to the farm. They stopped to rest by the sign at the farm's entrance.

Henry jumped off his bike. "I think this sign is even more crooked than ever," he said. "I'm sure I can fix it. I'll ask Mr. Beckett for some tools."

"Look at that!" Violet exclaimed. She pointed at a smashed pumpkin underneath the sign. "That wasn't there yesterday."

Just then, a speeding blue car turned sharply into the lane.

"Watch out!" cried Jessie. She pulled Benny out of the way just in time.

The car did not stop. The man behind the wheel blew his horn at the Aldens and raced toward the farmhouse. It looked like Jason. A cloud of dust followed him.

"That was dangerous!" Henry cried.

"Maybe he didn't see us," Violet said. "But he was driving much too fast."

The Aldens jumped back on their bikes and pedaled toward the farm. They were surprised when they reached the farm stand. Many pumpkins lay smashed on the ground. The beautiful flowerpots had all been knocked off the display stand.

Mr. and Mrs. Beckett, Sally, Jason, and Bessie all stood by the booth talking. The blue car was parked in the gravel lot.

"There they are!" Bessie shouted. "Those are the kids I was telling you about. They were fooling around with the pumpkins yesterday."

"Oh, Bessie, stop," said Mr. Beckett. "This is Henry, Jessie, Violet, and Benny Alden. I'm sure they didn't do this. They are our friends."

Bessie pointed a finger at Violet. "Well, that one there was snooping around in the booth yesterday. That's not very friendly!"

Violet's face turned bright red. "I was not snooping in the booth! I was only paying for the pumpkins we bought."

"Bessie," Mr. Beckett said, "please go in the booth and check that everything is in order."

"That's a good idea." Bessie paused to stare at Violet. "And if anything is missing in there, I'll know who to blame." Bessie pulled a large key ring from her pocket. She unlocked the door and disappeared into the booth.

Violet was so stunned she did not know what to say. She crossed her arms tightly and stared at the booth.

Mrs. Beckett put her arm around Violet. "Don't worry about Bessie, Violet," she said. "She is just upset by the mess she found this morning. We know you did nothing wrong."

Violet was angry at first, but she noticed that Bessie had seemed quite upset. Her eyes were red and puffy and her short hair looked messy and uncombed.

"What did happen here?" Henry asked.

"We're not sure, Henry," Mr. Beckett said. "Bessie found things this way when she arrived this morning."

Jason kicked at a fallen flower pot. "Maybe it was that pumpkin head ghost."

Mr. Beckett glanced at the Aldens and shook his head. "Jason, you know that there is no such thing."

"That's what you always say," Jason said, "but I know what I saw. Anyway, we'd better cancel the Girl Scout hayride."

Mr. Beckett sighed. "I suppose you're right. We can't have them come with the farm looking like this. It's a shame. We sure could have used the money."

"I will call them now," Jason said. "You go rest your leg."

"Wait," Jessie said. "When are the Girl Scouts coming?"

Mrs. Beckett looked at her watch. "In about two hours."

"We could clean everything up by then," Jessie said. "If we all work together, it shouldn't take too long."

"Yes," agreed Violet. "I can put all the flowers back on the stands and sweep up the spilled dirt."

"And Benny and I can pick up all these smashed pumpkin pieces," Jessie said.

Benny was already holding half of a pumpkin in his hand. "I've got the first piece!" he cried.

"I could fix your sign out by the road, too," Henry offered. "I noticed that it is crooked."

Mr. Beckett looked at his wife. "James was right," he said. "His grandchildren are helpful!"

Everyone got right to work. Henry borrowed the tools he needed. He carried them up the lane to fix the sign. Jessie found a wheelbarrow in the barn. She gave Benny a ride in it out to the farm stand.

Then they began collecting all the broken pieces of pumpkin. Violet was already busy placing all the flower pots back onto the display stand. Some of the flowers were ruined and she had to throw them away in the wheelbarrow.

"Hey, look at this!" Benny called. He held up a shiny necklace. "I found it in the grass."

"It's very pretty," Jessie said. "Maybe a customer lost it."

"You should give it to Bessie," Violet said. "She can keep it in the booth. Maybe the customer will come back and ask for it."

"I'll go show it to her," Benny called. He ran back toward the booth.

Benny was too small to see in the window.

He went around to the side door. "Bessie?" he called. When there was no answer, he slowly opened the door. "I found a necklace!" he called.

But Bessie didn't answer. She was lying flat on the floor!

CHAPTER 3

A Haunted Farm?

Benny called for help. Soon Bessie was resting under a tree in the soft grass. Violet placed a wet cloth on her forehead. Benny ran to get her a glass of water.

"I don't know what happened," she said. "I guess I fainted."

"It gets hot in that booth," Sally said. She and Jason had helped Bessie get up and walk outside. "It's one more old thing around here that needs fixing up."

Bessie tried to sit up.

"You rest," Mrs. Beckett said. "George will call the doctor."

"No!" Bessie sat up against the trunk of the tree. "I can't afford any more doctor bills. I am fine."

A big, black car drove up the lane and parked in the lot. A man in a dark suit got out.

"Looks like there's been some trouble here," the man said.

Jessie noticed that the man did not look concerned about the trouble. He seemed happy as he looked at the wheelbarrow full of broken pumpkins.

Benny handed Bessie the glass of water. Her hand began to shake when the man looked down at her.

"There's no trouble here we can't take care of on our own!" Jason said angrily. "You should mind your own business."

"Jason is right, Mr. Bolger," Mr. Beckett said. "You are wasting your time here. I will never sell my farm to you."

Mr. Bolger smiled. "The Wilsons said the same thing. But they did sell to me. And one day soon, you will, too." He took a check out of his pocket. "See this?" he asked. "I will give you thousands of dollars right now just for agreeing to sell."

Jason's face was red. He walked back and forth in the grass. "Your money can't buy you everything you want!" he shouted.

Mr. Bolger handed the check to Sally. Her eyes grew wide. "Dad! Mom!" she said. "This is a lot of money! Won't you please think about it? You could buy a beautiful new home in Florida."

Mr. Beckett leaned tiredly on his crutches. "We've already thought about it, Sally. We are not selling to Mr. Bolger."

Mrs. Beckett put her arm around her husband. They turned away and walked slowly back toward the house.

Jason's hands were clenched into fists. "I think you should leave now," he said to Mr. Bolger. "You are not welcome here." He stalked off toward the barn.

Jessie looked at the concerned faces of her sister and brothers. "Let's get back to work," she suggested.

Henry and Benny cleaned up the pumpkin pieces. Jessie helped Violet arrange the flowers on the stand.

Sally turned to Mr. Bolger. "I will keep talking to my parents," she said. "Maybe they will change their minds."

"They will have to," Mr. Bolger said. "A lot of problems have been going on at this farm. Soon they won't be able to afford to stay here."

"How do you know about the problems?" Sally asked. "How do you know what they can afford?"

Mr. Bolger winked at Sally. "Oh, word gets around," he said.

Suddenly Bessie groaned and held her head.

"Bessie!" cried Sally. "Are you okay?"

Bessie's face was white and she was shaking. She tried to stand.

"Let me help you," Henry said.

Bessie grabbed Henry's arm and stood up. "Maybe I should go home," she said. "I don't feel very well."

"I'll give you a ride," Mr. Bolger said.

Bessie waved him away. "No! I don't need your help."

"But I insist!" Mr. Bolger said. "You don't live far and, besides, I wanted to give you..." He leaned close to Bessie and whispered the rest of the sentence in her ear.

Bessie looked surprised. She quickly got into Mr. Bolger's car and they drove away.

Sally helped pick up the rest of the pumpkin pieces. "It's nice of you children to help out here," she said. "My own children are about your age. They love their grandparents and this farm, too."

"We don't mind helping out," Jessie said. "We like it here."

"And your parents are very nice," Violet added.

Sally tucked her hair behind her ears. "Yes," she said. "They are nice, but stubborn, too. This farm is no place for them anymore. I live in a very nice neighborhood in Florida. It is important for my parents to live near me and my family. One way or another, I must convince them to sell this farm."

"It's such a beautiful farm," said Violet. "I can see why they don't want to leave."

Sally stood up and brushed the dirt from her jeans. "It is beautiful. But it is so much work. And strange things have been happening here. It worries me a lot."

"Like the broken pumpkins?" Benny asked.

"Yes, and…" Sally hesitated for a moment. "Other things, too."

"What other things?" asked Benny.

Sally crossed her arms. "All right, I'll tell you," she finally said. "My parents didn't want me to frighten you, but you should know that this farm is haunted."

"But that's impossible!" Henry said.

"I know!" Sally agreed. "It does seem impossible. But all I know is that something strange is happening out in the fields at night. A glowing pumpkin head floats through the air like a ghost. It has no body beneath it. It is very creepy. There are voices, too."

"What kinds of voices?" asked Violet. Her

eyes were wide.

"Spooky voices," Sally said. "They say things like 'Stay away from this farm,' and 'Leave our spirits in peace.'"

Benny dropped a large pumpkin piece that was in his hand. He looked nervously around. "Has your farm always been haunted?"

"No," Sally said. "It was a peaceful farm when I grew up here. It all seemed to start about the time I came for my visit. Some of our workers have been so frightened, they have quit. My father can't even figure it out. He rode his horse into the fields one night to chase the pumpkin head. But the horse was so startled, she bolted. My father fell off and hurt his leg."

"That's terrible!" Violet exclaimed.

Just then a bus pulled up the lane and into the gravel lot. "Oh my!" Sally said. "It's the Girl Scouts. They're early. Henry, would you please run to the barn and ask Jason to get the tractor ready?"

Soon, girls in scout uniforms were everywhere. They picked up small pumpkins and gourds. Some liked the flowers and others wanted to buy the colorful Indian corn. A few leaned over the fence and threw feed to the goats. They were polite, but they kept the Aldens busy.

Jessie stood in the booth and added up their purchases. She took the money and made change. She sold the tickets for the hayride. Violet tried to calm one little girl who had been stung by a bee. Benny didn't know what to do. He had never been surrounded by so many girls!

The troop leader clapped her hands several times. The scouts became quiet and formed a group. They walked toward the barn where Jason was pulling out the tractor. A long farm wagon with metal rails was hitched to the back of the tractor. It was padded with bales of hay.

Henry helped the girls up and they took seats in the hay. The tractor rumbled away and the girls laughed and clapped.

Jessie stepped out of the hot booth. She wiped her brow. "Whew!" she said. "I can see why Bessie fainted in there. We should get her a fan."

"I wonder if the Girl Scouts brought cookies?" Benny asked.

Violet smiled. "I don't think so."

Just then, Mrs. Beckett walked toward them with a large picnic basket. "You children must be hungry," she said. "I made you some lunch."

Benny ran to take the basket from Mrs. Beckett. "Thank you!" he said. "Wow! The basket is warm."

"I made some fresh pumpkin bread." Mrs. Beckett spread a blanket under an old maple tree. "It's one of my specialties. I hope you enjoy it."

Later, after the Girl Scouts' bus drove away, Henry, Jessie, Violet, and Benny sat under the tree and opened the basket. There were tasty sandwiches, fruit, and a pitcher of juice.

Benny took a big bite of his sandwich. "Do you think this farm is really haunted, Henry?" he asked.

"No," Henry replied. "There is no such thing. I think someone is playing tricks to get the Becketts to move away."

"But who would do that?" Benny asked.

Jessie took a bite of her apple. "Mr. Bolger certainly wants the Becketts to leave. He wants to buy their farm so he can build houses on it. He could be trying to scare them away."

"I think Bessie is acting suspiciously," Henry said. "It was terrible how she accused Violet of sneaking around. And what was the secret Mr. Bolger whispered to her?"

Violet held a handful of grapes. She remembered something from yesterday. "The reason I went into the booth was that Bessie was not there. But I soon heard loud voices. Bessie was standing by those trees arguing with someone."

Jessie began to cut slices of the pumpkin bread. "Even Sally wants the Becketts to move. She said she had to convince them, one way or another."

"That's true," Violet said. "And she

admitted that the haunting started right about the time she arrived for her visit."

"And don't forget about Jason," Henry said.

"Jason? But he loves the farm. He told Mr. Bolger to go away," Violet said.

Henry took a long drink from his cup. "That's true, Violet," he said. "But when I went into the barn to tell him that the Girl Scouts were here, he was working on the tractor's motor."

"What's wrong with that?" Benny asked.

"Nothing," Henry replied. "Except that Jason said yesterday that he didn't know anything about motors."

"This sure is a hard mystery," Benny said, helping himself to another large piece of pumpkin bread. "It makes my head hurt."

Jessie smiled. "At least your appetite seems to be okay."

Benny put an apple on his plate as well. "Mysteries always make me hungry!" he said.

As they cleaned up their picnic, Violet noticed straw sticking out of Benny's pockets.

"What's that?" she asked.

"It's for Sam, my scarecrow," Benny said. "He might have gotten hungry while we were gone today. I can't wait to light the candle in his pumpkin head tonight."

CHAPTER 4

Scarecrow-napped!

When the Aldens pedaled their bikes up the drive toward Grandfather's house, they were surprised to see Mrs. McGregor and Watch in the front yard. Watch was growling and barking.

Benny jumped off his bicycle and ran to the post Henry had hammered into the ground. Sam the Scarecrow was gone!

"Oh, Benny," said Mrs. McGregor. "I'm so sorry about your scarecrow. I know how hard you worked on him."

"What happened?" asked Henry.

"I'm not sure," Mrs. McGregor said. "When I saw that it was starting to get dark, I thought I would light the candle in the pumpkin head. That way, you could see your scarecrow from the road when you came home. I thought you would like that."

"Could you really see it from the road?" Violet asked.

"Yes. When I went out last night, I could see it for a long way on the road. It was quite scary." Mrs. McGregor wiped her hands on her apron. "But when I came out this evening, Watch was barking excitedly. He had a piece of the scarecrow in his mouth. I think he must have pulled Sam down."

"But where did Sam go?" asked Henry.

"I'm not sure," Mrs. McGregor said. "Watch could have dragged Sam anywhere."

"Oh, Watch!" Jessie held her dog in her arms. "You silly dog. Sam was a harmless scarecrow!"

Benny sat on the ground. He pulled the straw he had saved for Sam's dinner out of his pockets. "I guess Sam won't need this now," he said sadly.

Watch had a small ripped piece of Sam's pants in his mouth. He dropped it onto Benny's lap. Watch licked Benny's face.

"It's okay, Watch," Benny said. "I know you don't understand about scarecrows."

"How about some dinner?" Mrs. McGregor asked. "It might make you feel better. And you must all be hungry after a long day on the farm."

"That sounds wonderful," said Jessie. "Thank you."

Benny rested his head in his hands. "I'll be there in a minute," he said.

Henry, Jessie, and Violet went inside to wash up for dinner. Benny sat by the pole with Watch, thinking.

"You have straw in your coat, Watch," Benny said. "And you had a piece of my scarecrow's pants. That means you must be guilty of taking Sam. But where did you put him?"

Watch barked and growled. He ran in

circles around the pole.

"Wait a minute," Benny said. "Something does not make sense." He felt around in the grass underneath the pole. The only thing he found was a few pieces of straw. Benny stood up. "Wait here, Watch. I'll be right back."

Benny ran inside and took a flashlight out of the closet. He jumped down the porch steps and into the yard. "Come on, Watch," he said, turning on the flashlight. "Let's go look for Sam. Maybe we can rescue him. I'll bet you know something, don't you?"

* * *

Watch barked excitedly. He ran toward a stand of trees at the far end of Grandfather's property. It was very dark, but Benny followed. He shone the flashlight through the trees and under the bushes. He saw two fat toads and a possum with a long tail, but no scarecrow. Benny walked deeper and deeper into the small patch of woods.

Mrs. McGregor put a steaming roast on the table. Henry, Jessie, and Violet helped to set out the mashed potatoes, green beans, and applesauce.

Grandfather filled all their glasses with milk. "That's odd," he said. "A table full of food and no Benny. Where is your brother?"

"I'm not sure," said Jessie. "I thought he was getting washed for dinner. I'll go check."

Jessie was back in a minute. Her face looked worried. "He's not upstairs," she said, "and he's not in the yard either."

"Oh, my," said Mrs. McGregor. "I hope he's not still upset about his scarecrow. Where could he have gone?"

Henry, Jessie, Violet, and Grandfather all grabbed flashlights and ran outside to search for Benny. Grandfather checked the back yard. Jessie looked in the garage.

"Benny!" Henry yelled. "Where are you?" Henry's voice was loud, but Benny did not answer.

Violet was shining her flashlight up the driveway. "Listen!" she exclaimed. "I think I can hear Watch barking!"

Grandfather and the children hurried toward the patch of woods where the sound had come from. "Careful," Grandfather said. They stepped over fallen branches and past prickly bushes. An owl hooted in the trees above them.

Suddenly Watch burst from the bushes, panting. "Watch!" Jessie called. "Where is Benny?"

"I'm over here!" Benny shouted. "I'm stuck!"

Henry ran. He found Benny by a wire fence next to the road. Some of the wire had come loose and was on the ground. Benny's foot was tangled in it!

"I didn't see the wire," Benny explained. "It was dark. And then I stepped into it. But look what I found!" He pointed to a pile of straw on the ground.

A round circle of blood stained Benny's sock. Grandfather worked Benny free from the wire and carried him home.

Mrs. McGregor stood nervously on the porch. "Thank goodness he's safe!" she exclaimed. When she saw the blood on Benny's leg, she hurried to get the first aid kit.

Inside, Jessie washed Benny's cut and put a bandage over it. "You should never go that close to the road, Benny," she said. "It's too dangerous. We were so worried."

"I'm sorry," Benny said. "I didn't mean to worry you. I wanted to find Sam. I thought maybe Watch knew where he was."

"Sam?" Grandfather asked, as they all sat down to dinner. "Do you mean your scarecrow?"

"Yes." Benny explained how they had come home to find the scarecrow missing. "At first, we all thought Watch did it. But he didn't! Watch is innocent!"

"How can he be innocent?" asked Violet. "Watch had a piece of Sam's pants in his mouth."

"I know." Benny scooped a mountain of mashed potatoes onto his plate. "But remember all the broken pumpkins at the Beckett farm today?"

"Of course," Violet answered.

"It made me think. If Watch had pulled down my scarecrow, wouldn't the pumpkin head have fallen onto the ground?" Benny poured gravy over his potatoes. "And when pumpkins fall to the ground, they break open. Watch could never have cleaned up all the pieces of a broken pumpkin head."

"That's true," Henry said. "I never thought of that. Good detective work, Benny!"

"But why did you go into the woods?" Jessie asked. She handed Benny a napkin. Gravy was running down his chin.

"Since Watch had a piece of Sam's pants, I thought that he might know where Sam was. We searched everywhere. I followed Watch to the fence. Something there made him bark a lot. I found some of Sam's straw on the ground by the fence. Then I got stuck." Benny rubbed his sore leg.

"Looks like you have another mystery on your hands," said Grandfather.

"One thing is for sure," Henry said. "Scarecrows cannot get down from their posts all by themselves."

"That's right," said Benny. "Even the scarecrow in 'The Wizard of Oz' needed Dorothy's help! And he could talk!"

"But if Watch did not pull Sam down, who did?" Jessie tapped her fork on the table. "And who would want to steal a scarecrow?"

Violet rested her arms on the table and leaned toward her brother. "Benny," she said, "I think Sam has been kidnapped!"

"No, Violet," Benny said. "He's been scarecrow-napped!"

CHAPTER 5

Violet's Fliers

Early the next morning Henry, Jessie, Violet, and Benny rode their bicycles to the farm.

"You did a good job fixing the sign, Henry," Jessie said as they rested at the end of the farm lane. "It looks straight and sturdy now."

"Thanks," Henry said. "But what is that on the sign?"

Someone had painted an angry pumpkin face at the top of the sign. Underneath it said, *Stay Away! Or Else!*

The children quickly pedaled down the lane. Bessie was just opening up the booth. The children were relieved that nothing seemed to have been disturbed at the farm stand.

Mrs. Beckett smiled and called to the children from her front porch. "Come on up to the house! I have something for you."

A tray of freshly baked cranberry muffins and a pitcher of cold milk sat on the table. Mr. Beckett rested in a chair with an account book on his lap. He wrote numbers in columns. There were dark circles under his eyes. Sally leaned against the porch rail with a cup of coffee and a newspaper in her hands.

"Good morning!" said Mrs. Beckett. "Please help yourselves to some muffins. They're still warm."

"Oh, boy!" said Benny. "I love muffins."

Henry, Jessie, Violet, and Benny thanked Mrs. Beckett. They each took a muffin and a glass of milk.

"I don't know if you noticed," Henry said, "but someone wrote on your sign up by the road."

Sally gulped her coffee. "Oh, no!" she said. "What did they write?"

Henry explained what they had seen. Sally's face went white.

"Don't worry," Henry said. "I can clean it off for you."

"Thank you," said Sally. "But it's worse than you think."

Mr. Beckett dropped his papers into his lap. "It's nothing but nonsense," he said.

"Maybe so," Sally agreed. "But some people believe it. It is scary. And now that more workers have quit, how will you ever run the haunted hayrides?"

"We do need the money from those haunted hayrides, George." Mrs. Beckett wrung her hands together. "I don't know what we'll do without it."

"Did something happen last night?" asked Henry.

"Yes, and it was very frightening." Bessie walked up the porch steps. She poured herself a cup of coffee.

"We saw a new pumpkin head floating

through the fields last night," Sally explained. "It had a very scary face. It glowed in the dark."

"It also made horrible screaming noises." Bessie shuddered. "And it warned people to stay away from the farm."

"Our employees were frightened," Mrs. Beckett said. "They quit and we had to cancel the haunted hayride. We have no workers left."

Benny's eyes were wide. Jessie knew he was thinking of ghosts. She put her arm around her little brother.

Henry had a hunch about the glowing pumpkin head. He wished he had seen it. "We could help out tonight," he offered. "It would be fun to be part of a haunted hayride."

"But who will come to our hayrides after this article in the paper?" Sally asked. She pointed to the headline: *Strange Happenings at Local Farm*. "The story says our farm is haunted. It says that our employees have quit because they are afraid."

"It's in the paper?" Bessie put her hand

to her mouth. "I didn't think he…" Bessie did not finish her sentence. "I have to get to work," she said. "Remember, Mae, I have an appointment later today." She quickly headed toward the farm stand.

Mrs. Beckett sighed. She began to collect the dishes and coffee cups. Mr. Beckett crossed out some numbers in his account book. "I suppose we'll have to shut down," he said. "Sally is right. Who will come to the farm now?"

"Wait a minute," Henry said. "Maybe the newspaper article will bring more customers to the farm. After all, don't people expect strange happenings on a haunted hayride? Maybe they will want to come and see this scary pumpkin head."

"That makes a lot of sense," Violet said. "I think we should make fliers. We can advertise how scary the hayride will be."

"What a great idea." Jessie smiled at her younger sister. "Violet is very talented. She could design the fliers. We could put them up all around Greenfield. After seeing them,

I bet a lot of people will want to come for the hayrides!"

"What do you think, Mae?" Mr. Beckett asked his wife.

"I think the Alden children are very clever! Let's give it a try." Mrs. Beckett opened the screen door. "Come on inside. I have some art supplies in the closet."

"And I'll drive you into town when the flier is ready," Sally said. "That will be quicker than riding your bikes."

Violet got right to work on designing the flier. Jessie suggested using bright autumn colors. Henry thought that drawing a few ghosts and the scary pumpkin head would be a good idea. At the bottom, Violet added a phone number and directions to the farm.

Benny was hard at work with his own paper and crayons. "How do you spell 'pumpkin head'?" asked Benny. "How do you spell 'scarecrow'?" He was just learning how to read and write. Jessie spelled the big words for him.

Benny jumped up from the table. "There!"

he said. "I made my own flier." He held it up for his brother and sisters. He had drawn a picture of Sam. Underneath were the words *Missin! Pumpkin Head Scarecrow*.

Jessie smiled. "That looks great, Benny. Just one little mistake to fix." Jessie squeezed the letter *g* onto Benny's paper.

"I'm going to put my flier up in Greenfield, too," Benny said. "Maybe somebody has seen Sam."

Henry was about to say something about his hunch when Sally came into the room. "All ready?" she asked.

It was a beautiful, warm day. Sally and the children climbed into the car to head for town. Some customers were already at the farm stand buying tomatoes and corn.

"Do you miss the farm when you are in Florida?" asked Jessie.

"A little bit. Mostly, I miss my parents," said Sally. "I was never much good as a farmer. I prefer to work in an office. Jason was always more help to my parents than I was."

"Jason?" asked Henry.

"Yes," Sally explained. "Jason and I have been friends since we were little children. He has always loved the Beckett farm. He would come over to play with me, but he would soon be out in the fields with my father. I think Jason was helping with the planting when he was only ten years old!" Sally laughed. "I hated to get my shoes dirty! I never went out into the fields. Even the mice in the barn scared me! I was never meant to be a farmer."

"But mice aren't scary!" Benny said. "They can't hurt you."

Sally shivered. "I suppose you're right, Benny. Maybe it's just that I don't like them very much."

"That's like our dog, Watch," Benny said. "I told him that scarecrows weren't dangerous, but he was still afraid. Do you want to see Sam?" Benny held up his drawing.

Sally pulled into a parking space in front of the office store. When she looked at Benny's drawing, a funny look crossed her face.

"Sally!" A woman in a green dress waved at the car.

"Excuse me, children," Sally said. "That is an old friend of mine. How about we meet back here in a few hours?" she asked.

"Of course," Jessie said.

Henry, Jessie, Violet, and Benny headed into the store to make copies of their fliers. They each took a handful and began to walk down Main Street. They stopped in many offices and stores to ask if they could tape a flier in the window. Most people were very kind and gave permission. Several admired Violet's drawing. They said that the haunted hayride sounded like a lot of fun.

At the end of one long block, Benny stopped. "My feet hurt," he said. "Are we almost done?"

"Yes," Jessie said. "Then we'll get a cool drink and rest. Do you think you can make it a little farther?"

Before Benny could answer, the Aldens heard a commotion close by.

"What's that?" asked Violet.

Two men were across the street. They were standing in front of a small café. They were having a loud argument.

Jessie grabbed Henry's arm. "Look!" she said. "That's Jason!"

"I could have been killed!" shouted a man in a blue shirt.

"I already said I was sorry." Jason had a bright red folder tucked under his arm. He accidentally dropped it. Papers spilled onto the sidewalk. "Now look what you made me do! Why don't you leave me alone? It is over now."

The man's face was very red. "I am still upset. You need to learn how to drive!"

People on the street were staring. A policeman stopped to ask if everything was okay.

"He almost got me killed!" the man shouted. "He stopped his car in the middle of the road! You should give him a ticket!"

The police officer looked around. Traffic was moving fine along Main Street. He seemed confused. "What car?" he asked.

"Oh, forget it!" The angry man stalked off.

The police officer shrugged his shoulders. Jason shook his head. He pulled a pen out of his pocket and clipped it to the red folder. Then he opened the door of the café and went inside.

Jessie looked at her sister and brothers. "I wonder what that was all about."

"I don't know," Violet said. "But that man was very angry. Maybe Jason ran out of gas and had to stop in the road somewhere."

Benny sank to the sidewalk. "I think my feet are out of gas."

Henry smiled. "Can they make it one more block to the diner? It's our last stop."

"Maybe they can make it," Benny said. "Will we get something to eat there?"

"Yes," Jessie said. "I think we could all use a rest and a bite to eat."

Benny jumped up. "Then my feet have just enough gas left!"

The diner wasn't crowded and the children slipped into a booth by the front window. They ordered sandwiches and four tall lemonades. Their waitress's name was Kim.

She had short blond hair and a big smile.

When Kim brought the food, Jessie showed her the flier. "May we hang up this flier in the diner?" she asked

"That is a beautiful drawing," Kim said. "I can hang it on the wall up front. More people will see it that way. This hayride sounds like a fun time."

"Thank you," said Jessie.

The waitress stared at the flier. "Hey," she said. "This is the Beckett farm!"

"Yes," Jessie said. "Do you know about the Beckett farm?"

"They sell wonderful vegetables at their farm stand," she answered. "And my friend works there. Maybe you know her. Her name is Bessie Unger."

"Oh, yes!" Violet said. "We know Bessie."

"Tell her I said hello," Kim said. "I haven't talked to her in a while. Is her husband feeling better?"

"I'm sorry," Violet answered. "But we didn't know her husband was sick."

"Oh, sure," Kim said. "That's why she's

been working two jobs." A bell rang in the kitchen. "Excuse me, kids," Kim said. "The order's up for table five."

After Kim left, Henry took a long drink of lemonade. "Two jobs is a lot," he said. "Bessie must really need the extra money."

"I hope her husband gets better soon," Violet said. She looked out the window at the shops across the street. Some people were stopping to look at the fliers. "Do you think the fliers will help bring customers to the farm?" she asked.

"I sure hope so," Jessie said. "I think the Becketts are counting on it."

Benny swallowed a big bite of his hamburger. "If the Becketts don't make enough money, will they have to sell the farm to Mr. Bolger?"

"They might," Henry said. "Mr. Bolger seems to have a lot of money and he really wants their land."

"Do you think he is behind all the problems on the farm?" asked Violet.

"He could be," said Jessie. "He wants

the farm very badly and the Becketts have refused to sell to him. Maybe he thinks he can frighten them away or force them to sell."

"That's terrible," said Violet.

"Yes," said Henry, "but Mr. Bolger is not the only one who wants the Becketts to sell. Sally thinks her parents are too old to take care of the farm. She wants to convince them to move to Florida with her."

Jessie pulled out a small notebook and pencil. She often took notes when there was a mystery to be solved. She listed Mr. Bolger and Sally. They both wanted the Becketts to sell the farm, but for different reasons.

Jessie tapped her pencil on the pad. "Is there anyone else who could be causing the problems?"

Henry finished his turkey sandwich. "Jason knows the farm well and he lives nearby. He could be behind the hauntings in the fields."

"But why would Jason do that?" asked Violet.

"I don't know," Henry said. "I can't think

why he would want the farm to seem haunted. It's just that…"

"Look!" Benny exclaimed. He pointed out the window. "Isn't that Bessie?"

"And Mr. Bolger!" Jessie said.

Bessie had just come out of an office. A sign above the door said *Bolger Construction*. She looked nervously up and down the street. Mr. Bolger leaned out the door.

"Anything else, kids?" asked Kim, stopping at their table.

"No, thank you," Henry replied.

The waitress placed the check on the table. "I hope you enjoyed everything."

"Yes, we did," Jessie answered. When she turned to look back out the window, Mr. Bolger was handing an envelope to Bessie. Bessie slipped the envelope into her purse. She got into her car and drove away.

"What was Bessie doing?" asked Benny.

"I don't know," said Violet. "But she seemed happy that Mr. Bolger gave her that envelope."

Jessie looked at her watch. "It is

getting late," she said. "We should get back to the car. Sally will be there soon." Before she left the diner, Jessie added Bessie's name to the list in her notebook.

CHAPTER 6

A Haunted Hayride

Violet could not stop laughing. Benny had found a scary skull mask. He was running around the barn making ghostly noises. Jessie pretended to be scared, but she was smiling at her little brother.

"Here you go," said Jason, walking toward them with a bundle. "These are the rest of the costumes. You can each choose whichever ones you want."

Henry, Jessie, Violet, and Benny were in the barn. Jason was helping them to get ready for the haunted hayride. He laid all the costumes out on top of some bales of hay.

"Do I look scary enough, Jason?" Benny asked from behind his mask. "Do you think the people on the haunted hayride will be afraid of me?"

Jason frowned. "I suppose," he said. "But that's not what I'm worried about."

"What do you mean?" asked Henry, trying on a long, black cape.

Jason leaned against the tractor. He took a deep breath. "Don't you know? There is something haunting the fields of the Beckett farm. I'm worried it will come back tonight when you children are out there in the dark. It's very frightening. You shouldn't be here. You should go home."

Benny took off his mask. He stood close to Jessie.

"But that's crazy," said Henry. "There's no such thing as a real haunting. It is all pretend. That's why we are dressing up in costumes."

"At first, I didn't believe it either," Jason said. "But you will see what I mean. Whatever it is, it wants people to stay away from this farm. There was even a story in the paper about it."

"We heard that," Jessie said. "But we still don't believe in haunted farms."

"Suit yourself," said Jason. "But remember that I warned you."

After Jason left the barn, Henry, Jessie, Violet, and Benny went through all the costumes. Henry chose to be a pirate with a long, shiny sword. He put a black patch over one eye. He wore the long, black cape. Jessie was a ghostly bride with a big white veil. Benny liked the mask he had been wearing earlier. He found a skeleton outfit to wear with it.

"Can't you find anything, Violet?" asked Benny.

Violet sat on a bale of hay. "I am a little nervous about tonight," she admitted.

"You don't have to work at the haunted hayride," Henry said. "You could help Bessie with the tickets instead."

"No, I want to do it," Violet said. "I know

it's silly, but Jason's talk frightened me a little."

"It's not silly," Jessie said. "Someone is trying to scare everyone around here. We are all a little nervous."

"Let's go out and walk the route of the haunted hayride," Henry said. "That way we will know what everything looks like before it gets dark."

"That's a great idea," said Jessie.

The sun was getting low. Shadows crept across the fields. The children stayed close together. They followed the tractor path through the cornfields. The wind whistled through the dry stalks.

"Look at that!" Benny cried.

Scary scenes were set up in places along the path. Benny ran toward a small haunted house. A ghost swayed on the front porch.

"It's just a sheet hanging on a rope." Benny pulled the sheet over his head. "Whoooo!" he called.

Violet laughed. "Look at this," she said. "This is not a real house after all. It has no walls."

"You're right," Henry said. "It is a fake house. It only has a front that is held up by wooden posts in the back."

"I see another scary scene," Benny called. He ran up the path.

Four scarecrows sat around a table having tea. One scarecrow had no head.

"That scarecrow sure is fat," Violet said. "He must have had too many cakes with his tea."

"How could he eat?" Benny asked. "He doesn't have a head!"

Henry took a closer look at the scarecrow. "I used to have a shirt just like that," he said. "I wonder…"

Just then there was a loud rustling in the corn. Something was stomping around! The children stood close together.

"I'm sure it's nothing," said Jessie. "But maybe we should go back now. It is getting dark."

Before she finished talking, a large goat burst out of the cornfield. It almost knocked over the scarecrow tea table!

Henry caught the goat by its collar. "Looks like someone escaped from his pen!"

"I'll help you, Henry," said Benny.

The goat did not want to be caught. It struggled, but Henry and Benny led it back home.

Darkness now covered the fields. Warm, yellow lights filled the windows of the farmhouse.

Mrs. Beckett stood in the kitchen. "You're just in time!" she said when she saw the children. "I've just finished baking the cookies for tonight. You can try a few for me to see if they turned out okay."

Benny lifted a warm cookie from the tray. He popped it into his mouth. "These are more than okay!" he said. "They are great!"

"I'm glad you like them," Mrs. Beckett said. She filled a small bag with cookies. She handed it to Benny. "You might need a snack tonight while you are outside scaring our customers."

Jessie and Violet helped to put the warm cookies into baskets. Henry lifted the big jugs of apple cider. Two long tables were set up outside the barn. Mrs. Beckett covered them with orange cloths and the children set down the cookies and juice. Benny brought the cups and napkins.

Mr. Beckett and Jason were lighting a bonfire in a clearing across from the barn. Sally and Bessie straightened up the farm stand and turned on the lights in the booth. Soon cars and buses began to fill up the gravel parking lot and the big grass field.

"Looks like a big crowd is coming!" Sally called.

Mrs. Beckett smiled at Violet. "I think your fliers worked. I've never seen so many cars!"

While Bessie was selling the tickets, the children hurried into the barn to change into their costumes. They heard Jason starting up the tractor.

Henry looked all around the barn. "I can't find my black cape," he said. "I was sure that I left it here right next to the sword."

"You still look scary," Benny said. "I don't think you need the cape."

"Thanks, Benny." Henry handed each of them a flashlight. "Let's stick together," he said. "Ready?"

Violet had chosen a scarecrow costume. She stuck a few last pieces of straw in her hat. Henry, Jessie, Violet, and Benny hurried through the dark fields. They stopped at the little haunted house. The ghost on the rope creaked back and forth in the wind.

Henry shone his flashlight on a red switch. "This turns on the spotlight," he said. "We'll hide behind the fake house. When the hayride comes by, I'll turn on the light."

"And I will jump out," Jessie said. "Do I look scary?"

Violet shivered. "Yes, you do! You look like a ghost bride."

"What can I do?" asked Benny. "I want to scare people, too."

Henry handed Benny an old tape recorder. "Mr. Beckett gave me this. There are screams and scary sounds on here. When Jessie jumps out, you push the play button."

Soon, they heard the tractor rumbling up the path between the cornstalks. When the hayride came to the old house, Jason stopped the tractor. Henry hit the switch and suddenly the haunted house lit up. Benny pushed the play button on the recorder. The ghost hanging from the porch seemed to shriek as it swayed back and forth.

Jessie glided from behind the house in her costume. She raised her arms and pretended to grab at the people on the hayride. Many of them screamed and hugged each other. Then the tractor pulled away and the children could hear the people laughing.

"That was fun!" Benny said. "Let's go scare them again!"

The children took a shortcut through the cornfield. They came out next to the scarecrows having tea.

Violet shined her flashlight around the table. "Weren't there four scarecrows here earlier? Now there are only three."

"The fat one is gone," said Benny. "Maybe it went to look for its head!"

"I will sit in that chair," Violet said. "I will pretend to be a stuffed scarecrow. When the tractor comes by, I will jump up and scare everyone."

The hayride was soon there. Henry turned on the light and Violet sat very still. Suddenly, she jumped from the table, waving her straw arms in the air. Benny turned the recorder on and ghostly sounds filled the night. People screamed again and laughed as the tractor moved on.

"Finally, it's my turn," Benny said. The next scene was a pretend cemetery. Benny decided to lie on the ground and jump up when the tractor stopped. "I'll be a spooky skeleton," he said. "And you don't have to turn on the recorder. I can make lots of scary noises all by myself."

When the tractor pulled up, the motor turned off. "Sorry, folks," Jason called. "The tractor seems to be broken!"

Just then, Benny leaped to his feet. He growled and snarled at the people in his skeleton costume. There were lots of screams and plenty of nervous giggles from the hayride. Benny's hollered so much, his voice began to get hoarse. Benny finally lay back down on the ground. But still the tractor did not move on to the next scene.

"What's happening?" whispered Violet. "Why are they still here?"

"I don't know," Henry said. "I will go check with Jason to see if everything is all right."

But when Henry shone his light up on the tractor, it was empty! Jason was nowhere to be found.

CHAPTER 7

Benny Disappears

"What's going on here?" one man yelled. "Why aren't we moving?"

Henry climbed up on the tractor. The key was missing. "I'm sorry, everyone," he said. "Perhaps the tractor is out of gas. I'm sure the driver will be right back."

"I thought it was part of the joke to scare the riders," Jessie whispered.

"I thought so, too," Henry replied. "I don't know how the tractor could have run out of gas. The hayride has only just begun."

"Maybe the engine is not working again," Violet said.

The tractor sat just at the edge of the cornfields. The large pumpkin patch stretched out in front of it. The sky was cloudy and the pumpkin patch was dark. Suddenly, a screeching noise came from the darkness. It was very loud and creepy.

"What was that?!" Violet grabbed Jessie's arm.

"Look!" Henry cried.

In the back of the pumpkin patch, a glowing pumpkin head floated through the field. It had a very scary face.

"Is this part of the show?" asked Violet. Her hands were shaking.

"I don't think so," said Henry.

The pumpkin head floated closer. An eerie voice drifted over the field. "Beware! Leave this farm in peace!" the voice screamed.

The pumpkin head got very close. It seemed to float in the air with no body beneath it.

"How is that possible?" asked Jessie. "It is really floating!"

Benny tugged on Henry's shirt. "It's Sam!" he cried. "It's my scarecrow! Sam!" Before Henry could answer, Benny took off. He ran after the pumpkin head into the dark fields.

"Benny! Come back!" Henry yelled. But it was too late. Benny had disappeared.

Henry and Violet turned on their flashlights and hurried to find Benny. "Benny! Benny!" they called. The glowing pumpkin head had vanished into thin air and Benny with it!

Jessie shivered. She stayed with the customers on the hayride. She assured them that everything would be okay. But some were grumbling.

"Was that pumpkin head part of the ride?" a man called. "How did it float in the air like that?"

"I didn't like it," a young girl said. "It had a mean voice."

Before Jessie could answer, she saw a bright light coming toward them on the path.

Sally walked up to the hay wagon with a big flashlight. "I'm sorry, folks," she called.

"It seems that the tractor is not working tonight. I hope you don't mind walking back with me. It is not too far. There will be free apple cider and fresh baked cookies. We have a nice bonfire burning as well. You are welcome to toast marshmallows and warm yourselves."

Sally and Jessie helped the customers down from the wagon. Sally shone her big flashlight along the path and everyone followed.

"Where are your brothers and sister?" asked Sally.

Jessie explained about the screaming pumpkin head. "Benny ran after it," she said. "Henry and Violet went to find him. I hope they are okay."

"Oh my!" said Sally. "I did see the pumpkin head. It was here last night as well. It seems to float over the ground. I can't figure it out." She turned to look at Jessie. "But why would Benny run after it?"

Jessie stared nervously into the dark fields. "He thinks it might be his missing scarecrow."

Sally put her arm around Jessie's shoulder.

"I'm sure your brother will be all right," she said. "When we get everyone back safely, I will help you to look for him."

"Thank you," Jessie said. "I am worried about him and Henry and Violet, too."

Back at the barn, the customers quickly lined up for the cider and cookies. Many sat on benches around the crackling bonfire. Bessie was busy selling pumpkins and corn. Mrs. Beckett poured the cider and refilled the cookie trays. She waved to Sally and Jessie.

"What happened out there?" Mrs. Beckett asked.

"I don't know," Jessie said. "Jason told everyone that the tractor was broken. We thought it was part of the show, but the tractor didn't move. When we looked for Jason, he was gone."

"Poor Jason," Sally said. "He must feel so bad."

Mr. Beckett limped over on his crutches. "I don't understand what is wrong with that tractor," he said. "First the wires on the motor came loose. Now something else seems to be wrong. I'm sure I checked it just this morning."

"Excuse me," Jessie said. "I need to go look for my brothers and sister."

"I'll be right behind you," Sally said. "Why don't you run into the barn and grab another big flashlight. There is one on the shelf in the back."

Jessie ran into the barn. She quickly found the flashlight. She was standing in the dark corner taking off her bride costume when she heard a noise. Someone else was in the barn! It was Jason. He pulled off a black cape and threw it behind a bale of hay. Then he grabbed a gas can and ran from the barn.

Jessie did not have time to think about what she had seen. Sally was calling her name. She dashed outside. They had to find her sister and brothers first!

"Ready?" Sally asked. "I think I see some flashlights shining in the cornfields. Let's head that way."

Jessie and Sally walked through the fields. The dirt was soft beneath their feet. They did not see Benny or Henry or Violet.

"Maybe we should stand still for a minute," Jessie suggested. "Perhaps if we are quiet, we will hear them."

"That's a good idea," Sally said.

They stood quietly, but the dried cornstalks rustled loudly in the wind. They were about to move on when Sally held up her hand. Something was moving. It was coming toward them.

Sally gripped Jessie's hand. "I do not believe in ghosts," she said. "But I am afraid of mice. If it is a mouse, I might scream." She shone her flashlight on her feet.

"It sounds too big to be a mouse," Jessie answered.

Suddenly, someone burst through the stalks.

"Bessie!" Sally cried. "What are you doing here? You nearly scared us to death."

Bessie was so frightened she dropped her flashlight. She put her hand over her heart. "Oh my!" she cried. "I'm sorry. I...I...was just trying to see what was going on out here.

I thought maybe I could help."

"But who is taking care of the farm stand?" Sally asked.

"You're right," Bessie replied. "I should get back to the booth."

"Have you seen Benny?" Jessie asked.

"No," Bessie answered. "But I think I heard your sister and brothers on the path a few minutes ago." She pointed to her right. "If you run that way, you should be able to catch them."

"Thank you!" Jessie ran through the stalks. She was not afraid of mice, but she did not like being in these dark fields all alone. She remembered the warning of the shrieking pumpkin head. Finally, she came to the path. She shone her flashlight up ahead. She could just make out three figures walking close together.

"Benny!" she called. "Is that you?"

"Jessie! We're over here!" Benny called.

Henry, Violet, and Benny ran toward Jessie. "What happened?" she asked them. "Is everyone okay?"

"We're fine," Henry said. "We'll explain later. Let's all go back and get warm first."

The Aldens were glad to sit around the big bonfire. The customers had finally all gone home. Mrs. Beckett brought out blankets for everyone. Bessie carried a steaming pitcher of hot chocolate and a plate of marshmallows. Jason sat with his head in his hands.

"Don't worry, Jason," Sally said. "There wasn't anything you could do about it."

Jason shook his head. "Were the people on the hayride very frightened? Do you think they will stay away from the farm?"

"Some were frightened," Jessie said. "But I think that most had a very nice time."

"Yes," Violet added. "I heard one couple say that they would come back next week. They said that they would love to live in such a beautiful place."

"What?" Jason jumped up. "What a thing to say! They cannot live here. This is a farm. This will always be a farm!" He turned to Mr. Beckett. "We do not even need to have these hayrides."

"But the hayrides bring in customers and money," Mr. Beckett said.

Jason stood near the fire. Bright orange light lit up his face. "There are better ways to make money. This is a farm, not an amusement park!"

Suddenly, Benny fell off the bench onto the ground. He had fallen asleep next to Jessie.

"Oh, my!" Mrs. Beckett said. "Are you all right, Benny?"

Benny rubbed his eyes. "I guess so. What happened?"

"It is late," Mrs. Beckett said. "We can talk tomorrow. These children need to go home to bed."

"They cannot ride their bikes in the dark," Sally said. "It is too dangerous on these roads. Jason, will you give them a ride home in the truck?"

Jason stopped his pacing. "Of course," he said. He went to load the bikes into the back of the pickup truck. Henry carried the sleepy Benny. Jessie folded the blankets for Mrs. Beckett.

"I left my water bottle in the booth," Violet said. "I will meet you in a minute."

Violet ran to the booth. She could hear Bessie talking inside. "Yes, some people were frightened," she said, "but not everyone. Something much worse will have to happen to scare everyone away."

Violet did not want to interrupt. But she felt uncomfortable listening to Bessie's private conversation. She knocked on the door of the booth.

The door flung open. "Violet!" Bessie quickly dropped her phone into her pocket. "Don't you know that it is not nice to snoop on people?"

"I'm sorry," Violet said. "But I am not snooping. I just stopped by to pick up my water bottle." Violet pointed to the bottle sitting on the counter. "I am going home now."

"Oh." Bessie handed the bottle to Violet.

"Me, too. I was just calling my husband to tell him that I am on my way."

Henry, Jessie, Violet, and Benny were very

tired. It was hard to stay awake on the way home. Henry sat up front. He gave directions to Jason.

"Here?" Jason asked. "This is your driveway?"

"Yes," Henry said. "Make a left. This is where we live."

Jason seemed surprised. He parked the truck in front of the house. He helped Henry to take the bikes out of the back. When Jessie opened the front door of the house for Benny, Watch dashed outside. He began to growl and bark at Jason.

"Watch!" Jessie called. "Stop that! Come back!"

But Watch did not stop. He barked angrily at Jason.

"You have a mean dog," Jason said. "You should keep it on a leash."

"Watch is not mean!" Jessie knelt down beside her dog. "I am sorry that he is barking at you this way. I don't know what has gotten into him."

Jessie took Watch by the collar. She led

him into the house. But Watch continued to growl until Jason had driven away.

Jessie held her dog in her arms. Watch was trembling. "What is it, boy?" she asked. "What has gotten you so upset?"

CHAPTER 8

The Secret Room

Benny woke to the smell of warm apple cinnamon waffles. He jumped out of bed. The first thing he did was look out the window. There was frost on the ground. Red leaves were falling from the old tree out front. But Sam was still missing.

When Benny came downstairs, Henry, Jessie, and Violet were already at the table. Mrs. McGregor set a full plate in front of Benny. "I hope you're hungry," she said.

"A little bit," Benny answered.

"A little bit!" Mrs. McGregor put her hand on Benny's forehead. "Are you feeling sick? Benny Alden has never been only a little bit hungry."

Benny did not smile. He rested his chin in his hand. "I just keep thinking about Sam. I wonder if I will ever get him back."

"What happened when you ran into the fields last night?" asked Jessie. "Did you find anything?"

"I wasn't afraid," Benny said. "I knew that the pumpkin head was Sam. I would recognize him anywhere. I ran after him. The head was floating around and screaming. But there was no body. Then all of a sudden it disappeared."

"That's very odd. How could that happen?" asked Jessie.

Benny shook his head. "I don't know. One minute the pumpkin head was there and the next minute it was gone." He took a small bite of his waffle. "Why would my scarecrow keep running away from me?"

"Scarecrows can't really run, Benny," Henry said. "Someone is playing tricks. I think your scarecrow is somewhere on the Beckett's farm. If we can find Sam, maybe we can find out who is playing the tricks and why."

Jessie opened up her notebook. "Do you have any idea who could be playing the tricks, Henry?"

"It could have been Jason," Henry said. "He was not on the tractor when the pumpkin head was floating in the fields."

"That's true," said Violet. "But maybe he just went back to get help."

"Sally said that she saw the pumpkin head," Jessie added. "And then after it disappeared, she showed up with a flashlight. So it could have been Sally, too."

Violet poured syrup over her waffle. She remembered what she had overheard last night. "Don't forget about Bessie. When I went to get my water bottle from the booth, I heard Bessie talking to someone on her cell phone. She was mentioning how the customers weren't scared enough by the pumpkin head. She thought something worse needed to happen on the farm to scare people away."

"But wasn't Bessie in the booth all night?" Henry asked. "How could she have caused the trouble with the pumpkin head?"

"I don't know," said Violet. "I suppose you're right."

"No!" Jessie was writing quickly in the notebook. "Bessie was not in the booth all night. When Sally and I went looking for you in the fields, we saw Bessie in the cornstalks. She said she was there to help. But she was surprised to see Sally and me."

Benny finished his waffle. He did not ask for seconds. He was thinking hard. "Maybe it was not Sally, or Jason, or Bessie," he said. "Maybe Sam really *is* a haunted scarecrow!"

"But there's no such thing," said Violet.

Benny pushed his plate away. "Watch was afraid of Sam. Then Sam disappeared. Now he floats without his body. How can anyone make a pumpkin head float unless it is haunted?" Benny's eyes were wide.

Henry, Jessie, and Violet did not know how to answer Benny's question. The floating pumpkin head was a mystery.

When they arrived at the farm later in the morning, the four Aldens saw Mr. and Mrs. Beckett getting into their car.

"We're off to the doctor!" Mrs. Beckett said. "It's time to get a checkup on Mr. Beckett's leg. We'll be back soon."

"Good luck!" Violet said. "I hope you get good news from the doctor."

"Thank you." Mrs. Beckett put her husband's crutches in the back seat. She pulled a key from her pocket and handed it to Violet. "This is for the booth," she said. "Would you children be able to open up the farm stand today? Bessie has called in sick again. That poor woman has not been well lately."

"We would be happy to," Violet said.

Mrs. Beckett smiled. "Thanks to your wonderful fliers, we sold a lot of pumpkins and flowers last night. You may need to get more pumpkins for the farm stand. You can pick them from the pumpkin patch. The mum plants are sitting in rows beside the barn. Choose whichever ones you like for the stand." Mrs. Beckett got into the driver's seat. She waved good-bye as the car pulled away.

Henry, Jessie, Violet, and Benny headed into the barn.

"The wheelbarrows are in the back," Jessie said.

"Hey! Look at me!" Benny called. He had climbed to the top of a big pile of hay bales.

"Be careful, Benny," Jessie said.

Henry and Jessie each grabbed a large wheelbarrow. "I'll give you a ride again, Benny," Jessie said.

"Where did he go?" Violet asked. "He was here a minute ago. Benny! Where are you?" Violet heard Benny's muffled voice. "I'm back here behind the hay bales. Come and take a look. I found something!"

At first, Violet could not find Benny. Henry walked all around the pile of hay bales. Then he pushed a few out of the way. Violet, Jessie, and Henry squeezed between the bales.

"It's like a little room," Violet said.

"With hay bales for walls," Henry added.

"There's even a hay bale desk over here," Benny said. "It has a red folder and some papers on it, but the words are too hard for me to read. And there's a map, too."

"That's a map of the Beckett farm," Henry said. "There's the house. The fields are all marked with their crops. And here is the farm stand."

"I think I have seen that red folder somewhere before," Jessie said. "But I don't remember where."

Violet looked closely at the map. "Something is wrong," she said. "The farm stand on this map is too big and it is close to the road. The Beckett's farm stand is much smaller. It is closer to the house."

"And why are there pear trees on this map?" Jessie asked. "I do not remember seeing them on the farm. Also, the pumpkin patch is missing."

"Look what I found!" Benny was wearing a long, black cape and running around the hay bale room. "It's your missing cape, Henry. You must have left it in here."

"But I didn't," Henry said. "I have never been in here before. I only thought this was a big pile of hay bales."

"That's what it looks like from the outside," Jessie said. "Someone wanted this space to be private. We should probably not intrude here."

"I like it in here," Benny said. "It is almost as cool as our boxcar. I think we should build a hay bale clubhouse in our back yard."

Henry smiled. "That would take a lot of hay," he said. "But we should listen to Jessie right now. Someone wanted to keep this room secret. We should go."

"Can I bring the cape?" Benny asked.

"I suppose so," Henry said. "We can put it away with the other costumes."

After Jessie, Violet, and Benny left the little room, Henry pushed the hay bales back into place. The little room disappeared once again. It only looked like a big pile of hay bales in the corner of the barn.

Jessie took the cape from Benny and folded it. She was about to put it in the bin with the other costumes when she suddenly remembered something. She had seen this cape last night. But Henry was not the one wearing it.

"Look out!" Benny called. He raced past Jessie pushing a small wheelbarrow. "I am going to beat Henry out to the pumpkin patch!"

Jessie followed her brothers and sister out to the pumpkin patch. They picked the pumpkins from their long, green vines. They piled them into the wheelbarrows. It was hard work to push the heavy wheelbarrows through the field and back to the farm stand.

"Benny and I will unload these pumpkins," Henry said.

Violet and Jessie placed two dozen mum plants in a long, flat wagon. They pulled the wagon back to the farm stand.

"We are just in time," Jessie said. "Here

come the first customers of the day."

Violet remembered the key that Mrs. Beckett had given her. She quickly pulled it from her pocket. She opened the door to the booth and stepped inside. She opened the window. She set up the sign with the prices. The cash box was on a high shelf. Violet stood on her tiptoes. As she reached for the box, she knocked the shelf. It came clattering to the floor.

Henry ran inside. "Are you okay, Violet?"

"Yes," she answered. "That shelf was loose. When I reached for the cash box, I knocked it down."

"I will fix it," Henry said. "Don't worry."

Violet picked up the cash box. A newspaper had fallen to the floor as well. "This is odd," she said. "This is an old newspaper from last month."

Henry adjusted the shelf. He tightened a loose screw. "Maybe Bessie forgot it was up on the shelf."

"Look," Violet said. She showed the paper to Henry.

It was the "Help Wanted" section of the local paper. A red circle was drawn around one advertisement. It read, *Office Help Wanted. Good Pay. Call Bolger Construction.*

CHAPTER 9

A Plan

The farm stand was very busy. Customers were buying pumpkins and fall wreaths and fresh vegetables.

Sally walked toward the stand with a large basket of tomatoes. "I just picked these from the greenhouse. Do we have room for them?"

Jessie quickly made a spot on a table for the basket. "They look wonderful," she said.

"Yes," Sally answered. "Jason has a special talent. Everything he plants grows big and tasty! Every year his tomatoes are the best.

I use them to make sauce and I bring some of it home to Florida."

Henry was standing nearby. He was breathing hard. He had just carried a very large pumpkin to a customer's car. "He certainly grows big pumpkins, too."

Sally looked out toward the fields. "No," she said. "My father grows the pumpkins."

"Doesn't Jason like pumpkins?" Benny asked.

"It's not that," Sally explained. "Jason would rather plant other crops. I suppose farmers have different ideas about what is best to grow."

Henry unloaded more pumpkins from the last wheelbarrow. "What would Jason do if Mr. Bolger bought the farm and built houses here?" he asked.

Sally sat in an old chair next to the vegetable stand. "I asked about that. Mr. Bolger said that he would give Jason a job building the houses."

"I don't think Jason would like that," Henry said.

Sally sighed. "You're right, Henry. Jason would not like it. He has worked on the Beckett farm his whole life. It is a special place to him. I cannot imagine him as anything but a farmer."

Jessie picked up a few gourds that had fallen under the table. "When your parents are ready to sell, perhaps Jason can buy the farm."

"I've thought of that, too," Sally said. "But Mr. Bolger has a lot of money and Jason does not."

After her customer left, Violet came out of the booth to get some air. "It certainly has been busy today."

"Isn't Bessie here?" Sally asked.

"No." Violet fanned herself. Her face was red. "Bessie called in sick. She cannot work today."

"That's odd," Sally said. "I saw Bessie in town this morning. I went to the bank and she was walking down Main Street. She did not look sick."

"Maybe she was going to the doctor,"

Jessie said.

Violet and Henry looked at each other. They thought they knew where Bessie was going, but they did not know for sure.

"I have only a few more days on the farm," Sally said. "Then I must go home to Florida. I hope Bessie gets better before I have to leave."

"Your parents will miss you," Violet said.

"Yes." Sally wrung her hands together. "And I am so worried about the problems here. I must try one more time to convince my parents to move to Florida with me."

Just then, the Beckett's car drove up the driveway and parked in front of the farmhouse.

"Excuse me," Sally said. She walked away toward the house.

There were no customers at the stand, so Henry, Jessie, Violet, and Benny sat in the shade of the big tree. Henry and Violet explained about the newspaper they had found in the booth.

Jessie was surprised. "So you think that

Bessie is working for Mr. Bolger?"

"I think she is," Violet said. "Remember how we saw her coming out of his office when we were having lunch at the diner?"

Benny was munching on an apple. "But doesn't Bessie already have a job on the farm? How could she work for Mr. Bolger?"

"Some people work two jobs when they need extra money," Henry explained. "She might work at night or on days that she has off."

Violet leaned back against the tree. "Or on days when she calls in sick!"

Jessie remembered something. "Didn't the waitress at the diner tell us that Bessie was working two jobs?"

"That's right," Henry said. "I had forgotten that. She said that Bessie needed money because her husband was sick."

"I feel bad for Bessie," Violet said. "But do you think she is causing the problems on the farm? Maybe she is helping Mr. Bolger to force the Becketts into selling."

"It's hard to say," Jessie answered. "We do

not even know for sure if Bessie is working for Mr. Bolger."

Violet was staring at the booth. "I think I have a way of finding out for sure."

Violet was about to explain, but Mrs. Beckett was calling to the children from the front porch. "Come on up to the house!"

Henry, Jessie, Violet, and Benny hurried to the farmhouse. "Is everything all right?" Jessie asked.

"Yes," said Mrs. Beckett. "We are having a celebration lunch. We wanted you to join us!"

Mr. Beckett smiled at the Aldens. "In a few days, the doctor will take the cast off my leg. I will be as good as new!"

"That is wonderful!" Jessie said. "We are very happy for you."

Everyone sat at the table. There was crisp lettuce, fresh tomatoes, turkey, and warm bread fresh from the oven. Mrs. Beckett passed the apple cider around the table.

"I am so glad you are feeling better, Dad," Sally said. "But please promise me that you won't go chasing that pumpkin head in the fields. I don't want you to break your other leg. I already have too much to worry about."

"But I have to do something!" Mr. Beckett said. "I must catch whoever is causing all the problems around here. I want this farm to be peaceful again. I want our workers to come back. They will not come if they believe the farm is haunted."

"Do you have any idea about who is causing the problems?" asked Henry.

Mr. Beckett sprinkled salt on his turkey. "The only person I can think of would be Dave Bolger. But I don't know how he could do it. I know this farm better than anyone. How could Dave Bolger find his way through my fields at night? The person haunting the fields always disappears without a trace."

Mrs. Beckett passed a bowl of cranberry sauce to Benny. "But Mr. Bolger always seems to know what is happening on our farm. He shows up with an offer after every problem occurs."

Violet looked at Henry. She did not want

to accuse Bessie. She had no proof. But she did have an idea. She needed Mr. and Mrs. Beckett's approval. Violet shyly explained her plan.

Everyone agreed that Violet's plan was good. They would try it tomorrow when Bessie was back at work.

After lunch, the Aldens went back to finish their jobs on the farm. Henry cleaned the sign by the road. Jessie and Violet added more mum plants to the wooden stands. Benny set up the small pumpkins in row. Soon, the farm stand was clean and full of good things to buy. It was all ready for the next morning.

"We need to put the wheelbarrows back in the barn," Henry said. "Then I think we can go home."

Henry pushed the biggest wheelbarrow and Benny pushed the smallest one. Jessie opened the big barn door.

Benny ran inside first. "Hi, Jason!" he said. "We are putting the wheelbarrows back. What are you doing in the barn? Can we help, too?"

Jason looked surprised. He held something behind his back. "No! I am just...I was cleaning up these costumes. Someone has left them a mess. They are all over the floor."

"I will take care of it for you," Jessie said.

Jason mumbled a quick thank you. Then he hurried from the barn. The costumes were in a tangle. It looked as though someone had dumped the box over. Jessie carefully shook out each costume and folded it. She put them back in the box.

"I could have sworn that the long, black cape was here earlier," she said. "I folded it and put it with the other costumes."

"My skeleton costume is still here," Benny said. "Can I wear it for fun? I can scare Grandfather when we go home."

"I'm sure the Becketts won't mind," Jessie said. "There are no haunted hayrides tonight. You can bring the costume back tomorrow."

CHAPTER 10

Sam is Found!

"Look!" Benny cried. "Watch is afraid of scarecrows, but he is not afraid of skeletons!"

Benny was wearing the skeleton costume. He and Watch played in Grandfather's front yard. Watch jumped on Benny. He licked Benny's face.

Henry, Jessie, and Violet sat on the front porch. It was dark. The air was cool and crisp. Jessie tapped her pencil on her notebook. "Let's go over it one more time before tomorrow," she said. "Mr. Bolger wants the Beckett farm. He wants to build houses there. And Bessie is probably working for Mr. Bolger."

Henry nodded. "Jason loves the farm. He does not want houses built there. But he does not like the hayrides and the people who come to admire the farm."

Violet agreed. "Maybe Jason loves the farm too much. He does not want strangers riding through the fields."

"And he thinks Mr. Beckett has not planted the best crops." Jessie looked thoughtful. "I think Jason wants the farm for himself."

"Don't forget that Sally wants her parents to move to Florida," Henry added. "And Sally and Jason have been friends since they were children."

Jessie turned the page in her notebook. "I feel like there is a clue that I have forgotten to write down. But I don't remember what it is."

"What I don't understand," Violet said, "is how a pumpkin head can float in the air.

And how can it suddenly disappear? It seems impossible, but we all saw it."

Jessie stood up. "Do you see Benny?" she asked.

Benny had thrown a stick for Watch to fetch. He ran after Watch to the edge of the woods.

"I don't see Benny," Violet said. "But I see a small skeleton!"

The white bones on Benny's costume seemed to glow. The rest of Benny was hidden in the darkness. It looked like Watch was playing with a real skeleton!

"Now I understand!" Henry cried.

"What do you mean?" asked Violet.

"I will show you. Can you please light the candle in our jack-o-lantern? I will be right back." Henry dashed into the house. He found a dark-colored blanket in the closet. He brought it outside. He wrapped the blanket around himself.

Benny and Watch ran up to the porch. "Are you putting on a costume, too, Henry?" asked Benny.

"I am," Henry answered. "Stay here on the porch and tell me what you see." Henry picked up the jack-o-lantern and walked away from the porch lights. He headed toward the darkness at the edge of the woods. Then he held the jack-o-lantern over his head. After a minute, he blew out the candle inside it.

"Wow!" Benny called. "Can I try? The jack-o-lantern was floating in the air! Then it disappeared! That was spooky!"

"Just like the pumpkin head at the Beckett farm!" Violet exclaimed.

"Nice work, Henry!" Jessie said. "You figured it out."

Henry walked toward the porch. "I couldn't have done it without Benny," he said. "He gave me the idea."

"I did?" Benny looked confused.

"Yes," Henry said. "Your costume reminded me. Black things are invisible in the darkness. The pumpkin head haunting the Beckett farm seemed to be floating. But it was not. Someone dressed in black was carrying it. At night, we could not see the person."

Suddenly, Jessie remembered something. "Jason was wearing a black cape the night of the haunted hayride! I saw him slip into the barn with the cape."

Henry looked thoughtful. "I think we need to include Jason in Violet's plan."

The next morning, Henry, Jessie, Violet, and Benny were ready to put Violet's plan to work. They arrived at the farm stand just after Bessie.

"My goodness!" Bessie said. "This farm stand is in good order. If you children keep doing such a good job, the Becketts might not need me anymore."

Bessie carried her mug of coffee into the booth. She opened the window and set the snacks on the ledge.

Henry and Benny went to the barn for a wheelbarrow. They hoped to find Jason there.

Violet and Jessie acted as though they were tired. They sat under the open window and rested against the booth. Violet nodded to Jessie to begin.

"What do you think will happen to the farm, Violet?" Jessie asked in a loud voice. "There have been so many problems around here."

"I think the Becketts might sell the farm," Violet said. "They asked Jason to come to the house for a meeting at ten o'clock this morning."

"But what about Mr. Bolger? Doesn't he want to buy the farm?" asked Jessie.

"Yes," Violet said. "I think he does want to buy the farm, too. But I don't know if he knows about the meeting."

Suddenly, the door to the booth flew open. Bessie hurried out. "I am going to get more coffee," Bessie said. "Can you watch things here for a few minutes?"

"Of course," Jessie said. "Take your time."

Bessie walked away quickly. Jessie and Violet went into the booth. Bessie's mug sat on the counter. It was still full of hot coffee!

Henry and Benny wheeled some pumpkins to the stand. Violet explained how Bessie had overheard the conversation and then hurried away.

"Jason acted the same way," Benny said. "He looked really angry."

"He was in the barn," Henry said. "We made sure he could overhear us talking. We mentioned that we thought the Becketts might sell their farm to Mr. Bolger."

"Did you talk about the meeting?" Jessie asked.

Benny lifted a large pumpkin from the wheelbarrow. "Yes. We said that we thought there was going to be a meeting at ten o'clock with Mr. Bolger. That's when Jason ran out of the barn."

"What time is it now?" Violet asked.

Jessie looked at her watch. "It is almost ten o'clock now. Let's go up to the house."

Mrs. Beckett was waiting for the children on the front porch. She winked at Violet.

Mr. Beckett opened the screen door and limped outside. He sat in his rocking chair and looked out toward the farm lane. "I'm sorry, Violet," he said. "But I hope that your hunch is wrong. I hate to think that Bessie would do anything to hurt the farm. I know she is unfriendly sometimes, but she has worked for me for many years. I have always trusted her."

"I understand," Violet said. "I hope I am wrong, too."

Just then, a big, black car raced up the lane. It screeched to a stop in the gravel lot. Mr. Bolger jumped out and slammed the door.

"Look," Benny cried. "Here comes Jason, too."

Jason was hurrying toward the house with a red folder in his hand. He reached the porch at the same time as Mr. Bolger.

Mr. Bolger pulled a checkbook from his pocket. "Listen here, Beckett," he said. "I can pay you double whatever Jason is offering for this farm. You cannot afford to sell it to him. How much did he agree to pay you?"

Jason looked confused. "But I haven't....I thought..."

Sally walked out onto the porch. "What's going on here?" she asked.

"We're having a meeting," Mr. Beckett

said. "Can you please find Bessie? I have some questions for her."

Bessie stepped out from beside the house. Her face was red. "I just happened to be passing by," she mumbled. "I wondered what was going on."

"I think you know what is going on!" Mr. Beckett replied.

Mr. Bolger tapped his pen on his checkbook. "I am glad to hear that you are finally ready to sell this farm, Beckett," he said. "Now, please tell me how much you want for it. I have much more money than Jason."

"Who told you we were ready to sell?" Mr. Beckett asked.

"What does that matter?" Mr. Bolger shrugged his shoulders. "I have ways of knowing things. Maybe your daughter, Sally, told me. She visited my office only a few days ago."

Sally crossed her arms. "I *wish* my parents would sell the farm and come to live with me. But I did *not* tell you that they were ready to sell."

"It was probably those kids," Bessie said, pointing at the Aldens. "They are always snooping around."

"We are not the ones who have been snooping," Violet said. She turned to the Becketts. "Bessie has been working for Mr. Bolger. She tells him about everything that goes on at the farm. That is how he always knows when there has been a problem here."

"I don't know what you are talking about!" Bessie looked nervously toward the Becketts. "I have worked here for a long time. This farm is important to me. These kids don't know what they are saying!"

"We saw Bessie come out of Mr. Bolger's office," Henry said. "We weren't sure that she worked there."

"But her friend, Kim, who works at the diner, told us that Bessie was working two jobs," Jessie added.

"And then I found this newspaper ad in the booth," Violet said. She took the ad from her pocket and handed it to Mr. Beckett.

Bessie wrung her hands together. "You have no right to snoop through my things!" she shouted at Violet.

Mrs. Beckett put her arm around Violet. "Bessie, do not shout at Violet. She was not snooping. She found the ad while she was working in the booth doing your job. If you did not call in sick, Violet would not have been there."

Bessie collapsed into a chair. Her lip trembled. "I'm sorry," she sighed. "Violet is right. It is true that I work for Dave Bolger. But I have no choice. My husband is sick and I need the money. At first, I only worked in his office. Then, he asked me for information about the farm. He paid me to tell him when there were problems here."

Mr. Beckett shook his head. "So you called Mr. Bolger today and told him that I was ready to sell the farm?"

"Yes," Bessie admitted. "I overheard the girls talking about a meeting this morning."

Mr. Beckett turned to Dave Bolger. "You might as well leave, Mr. Bolger. I will never sell my farm to you, especially after all the things you have done to cause problems around here. I should probably call the police to report you."

"You cannot call the police! I have done nothing wrong!" Mr. Bolger stuffed his checkbook back into his pocket. "All I did was offer you a lot of money for your farm. You will be sorry that you did not sell to me!" Mr. Bolger stomped back to his car and drove away.

"What an unpleasant man!" Mrs. Beckett said.

"I am so sorry," Bessie sniffed. "I know it was wrong to give Dave Bolger information about the farm. But I didn't suspect that he was causing all the problems here."

"He wasn't," Henry said. "Mr. Bolger was telling the truth. He wanted to buy the farm. But he has not caused all the problems around here. Jason has done that."

Jason had been standing in the corner. He turned angrily toward Henry. "What do you mean? I love this farm!" he said.

Mr. Beckett looked very surprised. "Henry, I think you must be mistaken. Jason has worked on this farm with me since he was a young boy. Why would he do such a thing?"

Everyone turned to look at Jason. His face was quite red. He hung his head for a few moments. Then he looked at the Becketts. "You must understand," he said. "I love this farm as much as you do. And I never meant for you to get hurt."

Mr. Beckett looked very angry. He rested his hand on his broken leg. "But I did get hurt! And I lost a lot of money! Many customers were afraid to come here. Why would you haunt the farm and scare away the workers?"

Jason looked down at his feet. "I was worried that you would sell the farm to Mr. Bolger. I thought that if the farm was haunted, no one would want to live here. Mr. Bolger couldn't build houses if everyone was scared away. And then maybe one day you would sell the farm to me."

"It is a good thing not everyone was scared," Mrs. Beckett said. "It seems that the

Aldens do not believe in haunted farms."

"I tried to scare them," Jason admitted. "I slipped away during the haunted hayride. I was sure that the floating pumpkin head would frighten them. But instead of running away, they chased the pumpkin head. I had to disappear quickly."

"We were chasing Sam!" Benny said.

"Sam?" asked Sally. "I never heard of Sam. Who is he?"

"He is my pumpkin head scarecrow!" Benny said. "He was scarecrow-napped from in front of Grandfather's house. And then I saw his pumpkin head floating in the fields!"

"I'm sorry, Benny," Jason said. "I did not know that the scarecrow belonged to you. I saw it when I was driving home one night. It was the scariest pumpkin head I had ever seen. I stopped my car to look at it. I almost had an accident!"

"That was you?" Violet said. "We heard the screeching tires. We were worried that someone could have been hurt."

"No one got hurt," Jason said. "But it was

a foolish thing for me to do. I thought that Benny's pumpkin head would be perfect for haunting the farm."

"You came back the next day and stole it," Jessie said.

"Yes, I admit it," Jason replied. "But it was not easy. Your dog was very angry. He chased me all the way to the fence. He bit off a piece of the scarecrow's pants."

"That is why Watch did not like you!" Jessie exclaimed.

"I was surprised on the night that I drove you home from the farm," Jason said. "I did not know that you lived there. Your dog remembered that I stole the scarecrow. I guess he was trying to warn you about me."

Mr. Beckett shook his head. "I cannot believe that you did all those things, Jason. I am so disappointed in you."

"I'm sorry," Jason said. I thought that I was trying to save the farm. But now I see I was wrong. It is not even my farm. I will understand if you want to fire me."

Mr. Beckett took a deep breath. He looked

at his wife and she nodded back at him. "I suppose I should fire you, Jason. But you are like a son to me. You love this farm even more than my own daughter. What you did caused a lot of trouble. You can stay, but you will have to work twice as hard. You have a lot to make up for."

"I will work extra hard!" Jason promised. "I will pay you back for all the trouble I have caused. I have so many good ideas for this farm." He opened up his red folder. "Did you know that many of the restaurants in town would be happy to buy their vegetables from the Beckett farm? I have been talking to the owners. And here is a design I have worked on for a new farm stand. If we made it bigger and put it closer to the road, you would have many more customers!"

Jason and Mr. Beckett were looking through the papers in the folder when several cars drove into the gravel lot.

Bessie looked anxiously at the Becketts. Mrs. Beckett put her hand kindly on Bessie's shoulder. "Would you mind going back to work now?" Mrs. Beckett asked. "It looks like we have some customers."

"You're not firing me?" Bessie asked.

"No," Mrs. Beckett said. "I know it is hard when your husband is sick. It has not been easy for me with George's leg in a cast. But you must promise not to work for Mr. Bolger any longer."

"I won't," Bessie replied. "I promise. And I'm sorry for any trouble that I have caused."

Bessie hurried off to the farm stand. She almost bumped into Benny. He was kicking a stone around the front yard. He was waiting for Jason to finish talking with Mr. Beckett.

When Jason finally looked up, Benny asked his question. "Where is Sam? Is he still on the farm?"

"Oh, of course!" Jason said. "I'm sorry. I bet you want him back. He is in my office." Benny dashed toward the barn.

"Your office?" asked Mr. Beckett. "Do you mean the barn?"

Jason's face turned red.

"It's quite clever," Henry explained. "You

would never know that it is there. Jason made a small room out of hay bales in the corner of the barn."

"You do have good ideas!" Mr. Beckett said. "I wish you wouldn't hide them all from me."

"From now on," Jason said, "I won't."

"I have a good idea, too," Sally said. "With Jason doing such a good job on the farm, you and Mom can come to Florida and visit my family during the winter."

Mr. Beckett nodded his head. "That sounds like a fine plan. But then you must visit the farm with the children during the summer." Sally smiled. "I would love to."

Benny came rushing back pushing his scarecrow in a wheelbarrow. "I found him!" he cried. "I have Sam back!"

"Oh, my," Sally said. "That is the scariest pumpkin head I have ever seen!"

"And this is his body," Benny said. He picked up the stuffed shirt and pants. Some of the straw had fallen out. Sam's belly was quite flat.

"I think Sam has lost some weight," Violet said.

"I know! I haven't fed him in days!" Benny grabbed handfuls of straw from the wheelbarrow and began to stuff his scarecrow. Both Benny and Sam were soon covered in straw.

Jessie laughed. "One more handful of straw and Sam's buttons will burst!" she said. "I think he is full!"

"Who is full?" Mrs. Beckett walked out onto the porch carrying a warm applesauce cake and a pitcher of cold milk. "Should I take this back inside?"

Benny jumped up from the ground. "No! I am not full. Only my scarecrow is. I'm starved."

"That's what I was hoping." Mrs. Beckett cut big slices of cake for everyone. Sally poured the glasses full of milk.

Benny sat on the porch swing and ate his cake. It was soon gone. He was still covered in straw. It was stuck in his hair and on his shirt and pants.

"Benny, you look like a scarecrow again!" Jessie said.

"Yes," Violet agreed. "But there is one big difference between Benny and Sam."

"I know what the difference is," Henry said. "It is impossible to stuff Benny. He is never full!"

Mrs. Beckett placed another large slice of cake on Benny's plate. "Well, as long as Benny doesn't mind," she said, "I am going to keep on trying to fill him up!"

Benny dug his fork into the warm cake. "I don't mind at all!" he said, patting his stomach. "You can try to fill me up any time you want!"